The Seven Chinese Sisters

WRITTEN BY **Kathy Tucker**

ILLUSTRATED BY **Grace Lin**

ALBERT WHITMAN & COMPANY

CHICAGO, ILLINOIS

Also by Kathy Tucker:
Do Cowboys Ride Bikes? * *Do Knights Take Naps?*
Do Pirates Take Baths? * *The Leprechaun in the Basement*

Library of Congress Cataloging-in-Publication Data

Tucker, Kathy.
The seven Chinese sisters / by Kathy Tucker ; illustrated by Grace Lin.
p. cm.
Summary: When a dragon snatches the youngest of seven talented Chinese sisters, the
other six come to her rescue.
[1. Sisters—Fiction. 2. Dragons—Fiction. 3. China—Fiction.]
I. Lin, Grace, ill. II. Title.
PZ7.T82255 Se 2003 [E] — dc21 2002011330

Text copyright © 2003 by Kathleen Tucker Brooks
Illustrations copyright © 2003 by Grace Lin
First published in the United States of America in 2003 by Albert Whitman & Company
ISBN 978-0-8075-7310-5

Printed in China
21 20 19 18 17 NP 22 21 20 19 18

The typeface for this book is Hiroshige.
The design is by Carol Gildar.

For more information about Albert Whitman & Company,
visit our website at www.albertwhitman.com.

For my sister Mary, who can talk to dogs, and
my sister Barbara, who can talk to horses.

K.T.

To the Pans and their growing family.

G.L.

ONCE UPON A TIME there were seven Chinese sisters who lived together and took care of each other.

Each sister had shining black hair and sparkling eyes. Each stood straight and tall, except for Seventh Sister, who was just a baby.

But the sisters were very different.

Second Sister knew karate — kick, chop, hi-yah!

First Sister could ride a scooter fast as the wind.

Third Sister could count — to five hundred and beyond.

Fourth Sister
could talk to dogs.

Fifth Sister could catch any
ball, no matter how fast and
high it was thrown.

Sixth Sister could cook
the most delicious noodle
soup in the world.

And Seventh Sister? No one was really
sure yet what she could do, as she was so
little she had never spoken even one word.

Far away, across the bridge, through a forest, and up a mountain, lived a terrible dragon. One day he woke up very hungry. He took a big *sniff, sniff, sniff* and smelled something wonderful. It was Sixth Sister's noodle soup!

Down the mountain, over the forest, and across the bridge flew the dragon, straight to the seven sisters' house. The sisters were so busy they didn't see him coming.

First Sister was polishing her scooter. Second Sister was practicing for her black belt. Third Sister was counting grains of rice. Fourth Sister was talking to a stray beagle. Fifth Sister was throwing a ball up a mile or so and catching it. Sixth Sister had just stepped into the pantry to get some more noodles. And Seventh Sister was crawling around on the kitchen floor.

When the dragon peeked
in the kitchen door and saw
plump little Seventh Sister,
he forgot all about the soup.
Instead, he snatched up
the baby!

HELP!

Then he flew back over the bridge and forest, up the mountain, and into his cave.

But as soon as the dragon set Seventh Sister down — he was just going to get some salt — she said her first word ever. And it was an excellent word — it was HELP!

The six sisters had just started to look for Seventh Sister when they heard her call. Right away, they knew her voice.

"Seventh Sister's in trouble!" cried First Sister,
leaping on her scooter. "We must save her!"

The other sisters hung on behind. Pulled by First Sister, who was strong as well as fast, the sisters sped across the bridge.

Beyond was the deep forest, filled with many trees — so many Third Sister counted them by twos!

Now Seventh Sister's cries were louder. The sisters headed up the mountain and soon reached the dragon's cave.

They could smell smoke and hear the most awful roars.
Fourth Sister listened carefully. Dragons do not talk exactly
like dogs, but still she could understand a little. The dragon was
roaring, "There's no use calling for help — you're going to be
my supper!" and suddenly Seventh Sister shouted her second
word ever, which was NO!

BOW-WOW RUFF!

"If you don't bring her out, sir, you will regret it!" called Fourth Sister in the best dog language she could manage.

The dragon stopped roaring. What was that girl yelling?
All he could understand was, "Bring her out, sir!" But no
one had ever tried to talk to him before, and he was so
curious he picked up Seventh Sister and rushed outside.

Second Sister stepped forward. Then, fast as lightning, she leaped into the air, slapped the dragon on the chin, and shouted, "Hi-yah!"

The dragon was so surprised
that *WHOOOP!* — Seventh
Sister flew out of his mouth.

Back, back, back ran Fifth Sister ...
back, back, back and reaching up, up, up ...
she caught Seventh Sister neatly, like a
fly ball.

When the dragon saw that his dinner was gone, he fell to the ground, sobbing. "Hungry, hungry," he whimpered, and Fourth Sister understood him perfectly, because the word *hungry* is exactly the same for dragons as it is for dogs.

"He's starving," she explained, and now all the sisters could see he was quite skinny and sort of sad.

"Tomorrow Sixth Sister can bring him some soup," First Sister said. "But we've got to get Seventh Sister home. She's all worn out, and she needs her diaper changed."

"Sisters go home!" cried baby Seventh Sister, who was learning to talk very quickly now.

First Sister put Seventh Sister on her back and hopped on her scooter. The other sisters hung on behind, and they whizzed fast as the wind down the mountain.

But when they reached the forest, First Sister stopped. Now that they didn't have Seventh Sister's cries to guide them, how could they find their way through all these trees?

"Don't worry," said Third Sister, "I counted the trees when we came. We must go past five hundred."

And so, when Third Sister had counted five hundred trees (by twos), the seven sisters came to the bridge.

They scooted across and back to their house, where they had a wonderful meal of Sixth Sister's delicious noodle soup.

And what did Seventh Sister do when she grew tall?
She became the best storyteller in the world, and she always told this story first.